P9-CQP-804

GUESS WHERE I'M GOING FOR 3 WHOLE WEEKS??

CAMP DAKOTA

A FARM AND FOREST CAMP

Owned and operated by the Brett family for more than 25 years

With programs for girls between the ages of 7 and 14

► Swimming in our spring-fed pond

► Hiking and cave exploring — COOL!

► Nature study

► Daily horseback rides on our woodland trails

► Canoeing on Otter Brook

► Livestock to feed and care for

► Arts and Crafts

► Sports and games

I ♥ HORSES!

Campers create original skits for the all-camp show

THAT'S RIGHT!! I'm going to CAMP DAKOTA! (SLEEPOVER CAMP!!)

For my dad,

who has never, ever let me down

(this is **not** what I mean!) →

Come on, Dad, let me down!

Let's give Amy a nice, big hand!

Thank you again, Amy Shields, for being an endless source of encouragement and clever ideas, and for leaving such nice messages on my answering machine.

Ooooo... she's <u>OLD</u>....

Library of Congress Cataloging-in-Publication Data
Lewis, Cynthia Copeland, 1960–
Dilly's summer camp diary / Cynthia Copeland Lewis.
p. cm.
Summary: The diary of a frog-loving girl's first summer camp experience, from the rocky beginnings to the final, fun-filled days.
ISBN 0-7613-1416-4 (lib. bdg.). — ISBN 0-7613-0990-X (trade)
[1. Camps—Fiction. 2. Frogs—Fiction. 3. Diaries—Fiction.] I. Title.
PZ7.L584755Dk 1999
[Fic]—dc21 98-36182 CIP AC

← Good thing this is not "cm. p.", get it? ("See him pee!")

Actually, copying is **WRONG**!

EXCUSE ME! Have we **NOT** been to kindergarten yet? Last time I counted it went "12345"

Published by The Millbrook Press Inc.
2 Old New Milford Road
Brookfield, Connecticut 06804
(who are such nice people)

dilly's SUMMER CAMP diary

by ~~Cynthia Copeland Lewis~~

uh-uh! ←

by Dilly !!!

me, packing for camp

(see my cute frogs waiting patiently to see who will be chosen to come along....)

Awww....) so cute....

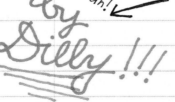

THANK GOODNESS!

Mom got me a new notebook JUST IN TIME for camp! My old one is all filled up with stuff about when my brother Matt was born. Now he's ONE ENTIRE YEAR OLD! And I am NINE- old enough to spend 3 WHOLE WEEKS at camp!

←LUCKY ME!

"Frog 3"→

COUNTDOWN TO CAMP ------------> JUST 3 MORE DAYS!

It will be SO FUN at Camp Dakota! Like a sleepover party that lasts almost forever!

I love sleeping over at my best friend Meredith's house. Sometimes we make a hideout in her bottom bunk by hanging blankets from the top. Then we tell SCARY STORIES...

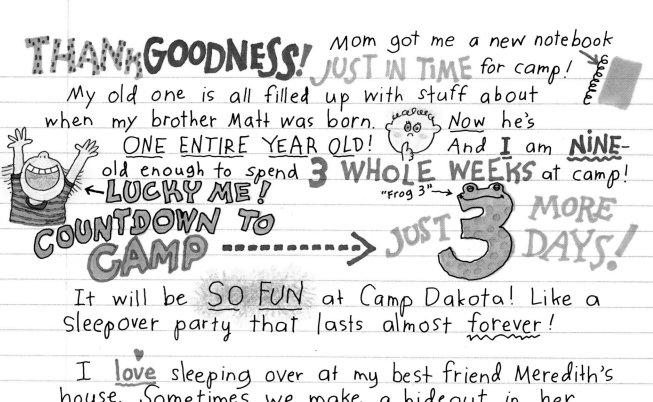

Today we got a letter saying Meredith and I are both in "Harmony" cabin!

Once upon a time there was a HEADLESS CHICKEN who always went to the graveyard during a thunderstorm...

CUT-AWAY SECTION LIKE IN MY SCIENCE BOOK

Once when I slept over we snuck into the kitchen at MIDNIGHT and made chocolate pudding and ate it before it got hard! YUMMY

Poor, poor Meredith

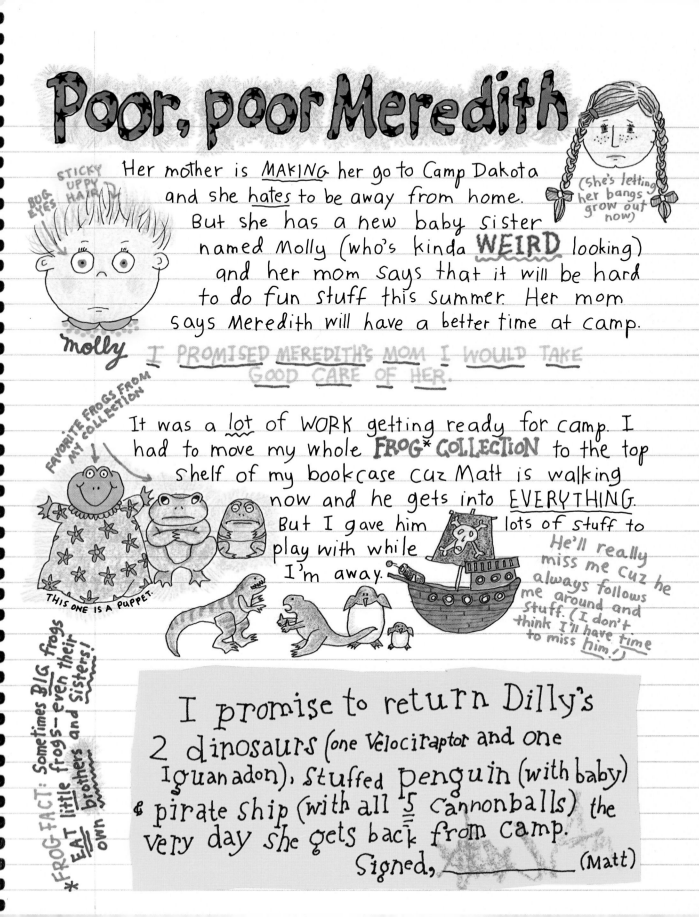

STICKY UPPY HAIR
BUG EYES

molly

Her mother is <u>MAKING</u> her go to Camp Dakota and she <u>hates</u> to be away from home. But she has a new baby sister named Molly (who's kinda <u>WEIRD</u> looking) and her mom says that it will be hard to do fun stuff this summer. Her mom says Meredith will have a better time at camp.

(She's letting her bangs grow out now)

I PROMISED MEREDITH'S MOM I WOULD TAKE GOOD CARE OF HER.

FAVORITE FROGS FROM MY COLLECTION

It was a <u>lot</u> of WORK getting ready for camp. I had to move my whole FROG* COLLECTION to the top shelf of my bookcase cuz Matt is walking now and he gets into EVERYTHING. But I gave him lots of stuff to play with while I'm away.

He'll really miss me cuz he always follows me around and stuff. (I don't think I'll have time to miss <u>him</u>.)

THIS ONE IS A PUPPET.

*FROG FACT: Sometimes BIG frogs EAT little frogs—even their own brothers and sisters!

I promise to return Dilly's 2 dinosaurs (one Velociraptor and one Iguanadon), stuffed penguin (with baby) & pirate ship (with all 5 cannonballs) the very day she gets back from camp.
Signed, _____ (Matt)

★★★ JUST 2
WHY I CAN'T WAIT TO GO!

1. I'll be like a grown-up, deciding what to wear every day, just like Pippi Longstocking.

2. I like having all of my things in my very own trunk. *Only I have the key! HA!*

3. Meredith and I already decided that we will share a bunk bed. (I get the TOP!) We can whisper all night about what our 3 wishes would be if we ever met a genie and stuff like that.

4. I'll learn to ride a horse and maybe my horse from camp will love me so much it will follow me home and we'll have to KEEP it! It can sleep in the garage and I'll ride it to SCHOOL!

me on → my horse

Wow! I have to take the bus!

I'm a walker. Dilly's lucky.

KID who rides his bike to school (He used to be THE coolest!)

5. We'll probably cook our food over a CAMPFIRE! And we'll swim EVERY DAY! (And I can even DIVE now!) Yummy! Bacon!

6. Maybe all sorts of forest creatures will become our pets like raccoons and bunnies and deer!

MORE DAYS!!

WHY MEREDITH COULD WAIT FOREVER
(cuz she doesn't want to go at all)

1. She thinks there will be spiders in her bed.

2. She can't braid her hair by herself → (or pull back her bangs)

3. The kids might tease her about Beth, her stuffed chicken. → sleeping with

4. The kids might tease her about her freckles (which Sam Horton always does in school).

5. She won't get to see "Arthur" on T.V. everyday, which is her <u>very</u> favorite show.

6. When she goes swimming, the crayfish in the pond might bite her toes.

GIANT TOE-PINCHING CRAYFISH

7. She will miss her toys.

8. She thinks she'll get hives from eating weird food like she did once when we had clams at the beach.

9. She can't fall asleep without listening to her "Party Tunes" tape and it says on the brochure "NO BOOM BOXES ALLOWED."

POOR, POOR MEREDITH

Camp Dakota Checklist

Please mark all belongings with permanent marker or tags.

- ✓ Sleeping bag/pillow — New one with ♥ on it! (Meredith's mother MADE her one with ♥s all over it!)
- ✓ Extra blanket
- ✓ Warm pajamas or sweat suit
- ✓ Rain jacket/rain boots
- ✓ Warm jacket with hood
- ✓ Sweatshirts/sweatpants
- ✓ Swamp shoes → SLIMY SWAMP THING
- ✓ Hiking boots
- ✓ Sneakers
- ✓ T-shirts/shorts
- ✓ Socks (heavy and light)
- ✓ Underwear (one pair for each day)
- ✓ Swimsuit and towel (ELVIS TOWEL)
- ✓ Bath/face towel
- ✓ Laundry bag →
- ___ Toiletries (including a bag for carrying them to and from the bathroom)
- ✓ Daypack for hiking
- ✓ Water bottle
- ✓ Insect repellent (no aerosols please)
- ✓ Sunscreen — NO PROB!
- ✓ Sunhat/visor/sunglasses
- ✓ Flashlight (with extra batteries)

This sounds DISGUSTING! (I'll put Mom in charge of it.)

Optional:
- ✓ Camera and film — LOTS OF FILM TO TAKE PICS OF ALL MY NEW FRIENDS
- ✓ White T-shirt for tie-dying
- ✓ Musical instrument (my kazoo)
- ✓ Spending money
- ✓ Stationery and stamps
- ✓ This diary!
- ✓ Markers and colored pencils
- ✓ A few little snacks and assorted treasures

NOTE: Pack ☺ T-shirt just like Meredith's!

Please do NOT bring:
- sandals
- dresses
- knives → Oh shucks. Guess I can't bring my machine gun either.
- matches
- boom boxes
- hair dryers
- video games → poor Mer.

Reminder to Parents
We encourage parents to send mail to the campers, as it is distributed each day. (Send it early so that it begins to arrive as soon as the camper does!)

HAVE YOU RETURNED...

- ✓ Your health forms?
- ✓ Your emergency and medical insurance forms?
- ✓ A letter saying: "Dilly Duncan hates cheese. Please see that she is given bacon sandwiches instead."

me, so excited I'm ready to burst!

JUST 1 MORE DAY!

TODAY IS THE DAY!

Hi DiLLy! ♡, meredith

Hi mer!

WE'RE ON OUR WAY!!!

← me ← mer her Mom

I'm writing this in the car so it's kind of BUMPY

OOPS! BIG BUMP!

Meredith's mom is taking us to camp (and _my_ mom will pick us up in 3 weeks). All of our stuff (except our pillows) is squished in the way-far-back. I hope the Skittles I packed are not all flat. ⊃ ⌣ °° {help!}

"DEE DEE!"

Matt cried when I left. I could hear him screeching "Dee Dee!" all the way down the driveway. Oh well. He'll miss me, but then he'll appreciate me more when I come home. I bet Mom and Dad will, too. (I'm a BIG help.)

Meredith and I are playing "Continue The Story" cuz she was crying and this is cheering her up. (Plus it's a L-0-0-0-NG ride. I hate car rides more than I hate CHEESE but camp is worth it.)

Once there was a lizard...

...And he married a princess...

...And the princess kissed him and she turned into a lizard, too!

...And when they went back to the castle, no one recognized them!

Oops! Another _wicked_ bump!

GROSS ME OUT!

Molly just threw up all over my pillow!!!

I'm writing this with a [flashlight] inside a sleeping bag because I can't sleep without my pillow. (Mer's mom took it home to wash it. Lucky her.) The one the counselor gave me feels like it's full of oatmeal and smells like old socks.

♪♫ sweet dreams ♫♪

I can't believe we just got here today. It feels like I've been here for 100 years. Maybe even 104 years.

~~Me and~~ Mer and ~~me~~ I were the last ones to arrive because we had to stop and clean up Molly's throw-up and that made us late. By the time we got here, the only bunks left were two bottom ones at OPPOSITE sides of the cabin.

Meredith started to cry →

Then MOLLY started to cry! →   "WAAA"

Liza, the counselor, took Meredith to the chicken coop to cheer her up. Meredith's mom took Molly outside to try to get those bug eyes to stop leaking. Another counselor told me to take the first bunk underneath this girl with a very big bottom. She put Meredith's trunk at the foot of the other empty bunk, under a very pretty girl with pierced ears and hair that has SHINY blonde parts.

Hi!

LOVE

PLUS OUR CABIN IS LIKE 29 MILES FROM THE BATHROOM (WHICH IS AN OUTHOUSE!!)

When I opened up my trunk, I found out that Mom had taken out ALL my good stuff!

gumball machine

favorite wig

Skittles

googly eye glasses

#1   key chain collection

Lucky pennies

hamster (in cage of course)

smiley face candle

MORE stuff Mom STOLE from my trunk!

And she packed my MERMAID bathing suit which I HATE because the straps don't stay up PLUS I haven't liked mermaids since I was seven or maybe even six.

DAKOTA
LIZA

when Liza brought Meredith back, Mer was all happy because they have DOMINEEKS EKES? or some other kind of weird chicken that she likes. (She gets to feed it every morning, just cuz she acted like a crybaby.)

(New and improved way to draw Meredith's braids!)

NOTE TO MOM & DAD

BULLETIN: I HEAR A WEIRD CREAKING NOISE.

I'm afraid that in the middle of the night, the girl with the big bottom is going to fall through the mattress and crush me.

IF THAT HAPPENS, MATT STILL HAS TO PUT THE TOYS HE BORROWED BACK IN MY ROOM!

We eat with the girls from all six cabins. At dinner, they took roll call and when it was my turn, Liza yelled, "Dolores Duncan" instead of DILLY Duncan just like on the first day of school. EVERYBODY laughed.

DOLORES? HA HA HA HA

AFTER ROLL CALL, WE GOT IN A LINE LIKE AT SCHOOL

Welcome to camp, girls! Would you like macaroni and CHEESE or a ham & CHEESE omelette Or a grilled CHEESE sandwich?

I LOVE macaroni and cheese!

me, too! It's my FAVORITE!

Nothing.

I'd better turn off this flashlight. It's making bugs come into my sleeping bag and now I'm bitten all over. SWELL.

I think all of this bad stuff is happening because Mom took my lucky penny collection out of my trunk.

I AM SORRY TO SAY THAT TODAY WAS EVEN "WORSE" THAN YESTERDAY!

*cold pancakes that tasted like ODOR EATERS with watery syrup

After breakfast,* we had our swimming test. In order to swim outside of this LITTLE TINY AREA marked off with buoys, you had to be able to jump off the dock and swim to shore, and then jump off again and BACK FLOAT to shore. Everyone passed the first part. Then everyone passed the floating part EXCEPT for me and this KOOKY girl from "Trail's End" cabin named Robin. I TOLD the lifeguard I could swim and EVEN dive, but all she said was that I couldn't go in the CANOE EITHER!

yucky swamp stuff

Meredith! Come play!

Let's play Marco Polo!

Robin

Beach

me with my sinkable body in my weird mermaid bathing suit

← Meredith and I wave to each other sadly across the buoys

I have a red mark on my middle toe. I think a crayfish bit me. But nobody cares.

AND JUST WHEN I THOUGHT THINGS WERE AS BAD AS THEY COULD BE ....

Guess what we had for dinner? PIZZA! – CHEESE PIZZA!!

me, trying to sleep on my oatmeal pillow

HELLO? Didn't I write a letter saying that I hate CHEESE? CAN'T YOU PEOPLE READ?

Meredith shouldn't have worried about her braids because EVERYONE loves to play with her long hair and they fight over who gets to braid it. Blah, blah, blah.

At lunch today (MY THIRD DAY IN THIS DUMP THEY CALL A CAMP), the "Fellowship" Cabin girls (who come EVERY YEAR— their parents must Really hate them) said that the "Harmony" girls are always weird. I think they're right because except for Meredith and me and the pretty girl with the shiny blonde hair pieces (whose name is Julie), they're a bunch of LOSERS!

CHECK THiS, though — Meredith doesn't even think they ARE losers — she LIKES them!

Mary Beth is the girl over me with the big bottom. She giggles a lot and likes to play Jacks.

This is Naomi. She has the "EEN" problem— like, instead of saying "I am going swimming" she says, "I am goEEN swimmEEN." It drives me NUTS. She also keeps whispering to everybody, "You're my new best friend!" Q-U-E-E-R.

Julie has dangly earrings, too.

I can't remember this girl's name. When she gets excited she breathes really hard and it sounds like she's snorting like a pig. I try not to get her excited.

Jessie sleeps under Naomi and cries a lot. I think she's homesick. Or maybe she's just a crybaby.

Paige always talks about her cat (like anybody cares). She has a cat sleeping bag, a cat pillow, a cat flashlight... Yadda yadda yadda.

(Paige also has underwear with the days of the week on them. Today she wore "Thursday" even though it's Tuesday. I think it's really going to confuse her later in the week.)

Hannah is like a boy. She hangs upside down off the top bunk and talks real loud. She has a pretty cool sleeping bag with glow-in-the-dark frogs on it. (She SAYS she has a little sister who looks EXACTLY like her. S-U-U-U-RE...)

Sylvia has her own horse and she's always talking about how great she can ride. She has this big clump of hair missing from the back of her head where her horse grabbed it and yanked it out. On her shoulder is a birthmark that looks like a galloping horse..... SPOOKY

O.K. I THOUGHT THE LAST 3 DAYS WERE BAD. (THEY WERE.) BUT TODAY WAS THE ABSOLUTE worst day of my life!

(including the day in third grade that Mrs. Bunn was sick and we had this TOTALLY MEAN SUBSTITUTE who made me stay in for recess just because I wouldn't be in a reading team with Blaine because he reads so S-L-O-W-L-Y that it makes me SCREAM!.......

GROWL

mean sub

This was ALSO the day they changed hot lunch from Chicken Nuggets to LUNCHEON MEAT!

THIS DAY WAS WORSE THAN THAT!)

I started out thinking it would be a FUN DAY cuz we were going to be assigned our horses. But FIRST we had to listen to this B-O-R-I-N-G horse safety lesson that lasted the WHOLE morning. Then at lunch, Naomi bumped into me and I spilled juice all over my shirt. While everyone else went to the barn, I had to go back to the cabin and change.

When I got to the barn, there were only 2 horses left to pick from:

SNORT SNORT

Hmmm....

CHOICE #2 "Starflight"

Pick me! Pick me!

(standing on tiptoes to seem taller)

CHOICE #1 "BUD"

STOMP STOMP

I think it would have been faster if I let Starflight ride me. (Joke. Ha, ha.)

At dinner (CHEESEBURGERS), Meredith was playing "Continue the Story" with Julie.

Right now is our quiet time just before bed. I am having trouble concentrating on writing this because Liza plays her guitar and sings to us. **EXCUSE ME, BUT ISN'T THIS CALLED "QUIET TIME"?** (Meredith LOVES it because it makes her fall asleep like her "Party Tunes" tape. (I miss mom.)

WHY MEREDITH COULD WAIT FOREVER

How about playEEN "Duck Duck Chicken"?

"SNORT SNORT"

Oooo Don't even THINK of asking me to play your dumb game!

CUZ SHE ♥VES CAMP!

1. She's too busy being *Miss Popularity* to miss her toys OR "Arthur." (Plus her Mom mailed her a bunch of "Arthur" books.) 📕📕📕 LUCKY.

2. There are no spiders in her bed after all. (They're all in MY bed.)

3. Dear Meredith, I miss you so much and so does Molly! She looks around as if to say "Where did my big sister go?"

She loves getting mail. **SO FAR:** 6 POSTCARDS 11 LETTERS NO FAIR!!

4. She thinks the FOOD is GREAT! (She even asks for SECONDS!)

5. PICK ME! PICK ME! She gets to feed "her" dumb chicken every day. AND she gets to pick somebody to go with her every time. (AND IT'S NEVER ME.)

6. She says she sleeps BETTER at CAMP because there is no Molly crying in the middle of the night and she likes to hear Liza's guitar. → 🎸 ♪♪

(Man, that kid would drive me bananas!)

7. She and Julie and Liddy (SNORT SNORT) and Naomi and Hannah are planning some dopey skit for the camp show. Meredith wanted me to do it, too, but I said I wouldn't be caught DEAD doing something that dumb. (Plus I could tell Julie didn't want me anyway.)

I think someone **stole** my markers. They all hate me. Poor, poor Dilly.

The roof leaks. ← See the water spots?

when I was looking for some clean underwear this morning (which I think I'm out of) I found my instant camera. I took some pictures just cuz it's raining and I have nothing better to do.

Meredith and all of her hokey friends having a good ole time. →

← mer

Julie

Hannah

I wish I was a frog and all my friends were frogs. REAL* FROGS I WANT TO MEET:

Ghost frog
Flying frog
Shoemaker frog
White-lipped frog
Pig frog
Hairy frog

* these are real frogs!

Naomi ↗

(Jessie lent me her red pencil.) ↓ **P.S.** The rain makes everything smell like my friend Beanie's dog after he's been playing in the swamp. → GOTTA GO. Mary Beth wants to teach me Jacks. I guess it'll be more fun than counting water spots on my sleeping bag.

Naomi found my markers under my bunk. I guess whoever STOLE them put them there. Of course, _now_ I'm supposed to be her best friend for the day. ᵒᵒ
(HOW THRILL_EEN_.)

EVERY DAY IS LONGER THAN THE DAY BEFORE. TODAY FEELS LIKE IT'S 5 YEARS LONG. BY THE TIME I GET HOME, MY PARENTS WILL BE ALL **WRINKLY** AND CROOKED

DILLY? is that you?

Mom →

← Dad

WHO?

I made this dumb bookmark in Arts & Crafts. It was sorta fun. Jessie liked it so much that she made one, too, only with lizards.

Swim time doesn't TOTALLY stink. Even though Robin never talks, she's not MEAN or anything (like you-know-who). Once she even _smiled_! Or maybe it was just a twitch.

Dinner _started out_ OK - no cheesy food _FOR ONCE_. Instead, we had watery soup with chewy chicken and mushy noodles. Actually, I _WAS_ going to eat it except that Hannah who was sitting across from me took a huge slurp and then spit it back into her bowl because it was too hot. That kind of made me sick so I just ate the crackers.

FROG FACT
there are 640 different kinds of tree frogs!

ptewg

↖ Hannah

| MAIL CALL | Meredith: 2 letters (including some stickers!) |
| | Dilly: BIG FAT ZERO |

At long last!!! FINALLY! A PACKAGE FOR Dilly

IT'S ABOUT TIME & 12 LETTERS and POSTCARDS!

Mom wrote the <u>wrong</u> zip code and my stuff went to <u>FLORIDA</u> before it came to <u>Maine</u>!

CONNECTICUT
LITCHFIELD
The Litchfield Green

Dear Dilly,
We all miss you <u>so</u> much – especially Matt! He keeps peeking into your room and saying "Dee Dee?" He can't wait until camp is over! Dad is painting a fish mural (with a few frogs, too!) in your bathroom. You'll love it!
Love,
Mom xo

P.S. Expect a package soon from Meem + Beep!

→ grandparents

← He's not the only one!

#17855 Photographer J. White @ Dorcus Photos
Designed and printed in the U.S.A.

USA 20

Dilly Duncan
% Camp Dakota
Pine Mountain
Gorham, Maine
~~33581~~
(03581)

*Recycled Paper

MaryBeth and I decided what our three wishes would be if we met a genie: #1. To be able to fly #2. To have a pet flying monkey #3. To get rid of EVERY SINGLE BOY!!!

This came today, too, cuz Mom gave EVERYBODY the wrong ZIP CODE!!

Liza let me share the cookies Meem sent with everyone in the cabin (but we were careful not to drop any crumbs cuz of the mice). Meem packed them in a laundry detergent box but everyone loved them anyway. (Well, <u>almost</u> everyone.)

← Snobby Julie

No thank you. They smell like they just came out of the washing machine.

UPSIDE DOWN FROG FACT:
Frogs blink when they swallow because their eyeballs help force the food down.

A TALE OF GOOD NEWS & BAD NEWS

good news! Robin definitely smiles at me now. She even <u>NODS</u>! It's actually BETTER than a real conversation cuz <u>I</u> get to decide what we talk about!

Let's talk about what it would be like if a Frog King ran the world, OK?

NOD NOD

BAD NEWS: Today Robin passed her floating test and now she is bobbing silently out in the deep water and I am all alone within the buoys.

the cheese-hater stands alone

yucky swampy stuff

MARCO... MARCO...

"POLO!"

"POLO!"

"POLO!"

"POLO!"

Polo.

FROG FACT frogs are grown up when they are 3 years old! LUCKIES!

good news! When I wandered by my all alone self near the swampy muck, I saw a FROG!! Then when I started pushing away the plants, I saw <u>2</u> more! I bet there are HUNDREDS! I was just about to catch one when swim time ended. But I'll get one tomorrow!

BAD NEWS: Right after swimming, we had "free" time but we <u>HAD</u> to work on skits for the dopey CAMP SHOW. I pretended to work on a script but really I wrote a letter to Matt.

REALLY good news! I just got a package from Aunt Ellen— she sent me a **REAL** WET SUIT! IT <u>ROCKS</u>!!!

like scuba divers wear →

NO MORE MERMAIDS

MAIL CALL

Dilly: 2 LETTERS
(including $5 to spend at the camp store!)

10? I LOST COUNT!
~~9~~ days left!

I couldn't *wait* for today...

CAVE EXPLORING DAY!

All week Meredith **PROMISED** she would sit with me on the bus. She *did* sit next to me, but she spent the WHOLE TIME playing with Julie across the aisle. But then I realized that Hannah was behind me and we played "Name That Tune." Pretty soon the whole bus was playing! (Even Julie!)

me

mer

Liza did her hair in tons of little braids

Julie

The cave was **AWESOME**!! It was called **DEAD MAN'S CAVE** cuz somebody found a real **SKELETON** in it a long time ago. We went way deep inside, when ALL OF A SUDDEN everything got **PITCH DARK**! One of the counselors said, "Oh no! Our flashlight batteries went out!" Everyone started **SCREAMING** except me (one of the Fellowship girls told me they play the same trick every year so I was ready). I could find Paige because of her glow-in-the-dark shirt. She was crying until I told her it was a joke. Then I heard Liddy snorting nervously and I told her, too. (Then we all laughed until the counselor turned the flashlight back on.)

Jessie doesn't cry at night anymore, which I'm really glad about. It kind of made me want to cry just hearing her.

When we got back, Jessie and I went to the pond and heard TONS of frogs plopping into the water. It was too dark to catch any, but we're going to tomorrow. And I promised Jessie we'd look for salamanders, too!

HEADLINE NEWS

Dilly passes floating test but decides to stay in shallow frog water... and catches loads of frogs !!!

Will it bite?

He's quite an attractive frog!

Can I touch it?

I hate frogs. They give you warts.

Frog Fact: No they don't!!

← Hannah is AFRAID of frogs! (I don't know HOW she crawls into that frog sleeping bag every night!)

I caught two right away! Jessie held them while I got my camera (and then she took a picture of Meredith and me holding them— and Hannah being grossed out!)

Today Meredith picked ME to help feed her chicken! ☺

Liza showed me a big terrarium in the Dining Hall where we could keep them for a few days. There are mossy rocks and a little pond. Liza fed the frogs hamburger on a toothpick and they took it!

Frog Fact: Frogs sometimes use their front legs to clean off their food before they eat it!

At dinner, Jessie traded me her corn for my ~~brocoli~~ broccoli(?) covered with CHEESE! She (Jessie's favorite) loves cheese (It's her only fault.)

☆ We couldn't find any salamanders today, but we will before camp is over!

⋆★ FROGS RULE !! ★⋆

Now EVERYBODY wants to stay in the shallow water with me and catch FROGS! (Except Julie, of course 👓) I caught enough frogs so that everyone could hold one!

frog bouquet

Jessie and ~~me~~ I are the only ones who can catch them! Jessie said that at home she has an 2 Geckos and a SKINK! Iguana

She ♥VES reptiles (like lizards) and amphibians (like frogs). We should start a FROG CLUB because we're the HERPETOLOGISTS* (Meredith said if we did start one she wanted to be vice-president. I said, "Great!")
*frog experts!

I finally got an idea for the camp show! But I told her it HAS to be a SECRET cuz funny stuff is only funny the FIRST time you hear it. Liza liked it a lot.

Hannah almost
← threw up when Liddy took my picture!
Silly Hannah!

Lollipop from Auntie Betty ↓

DINNER!
B.L.T.s!!! My favorite! (Actually "B"s are my favorite but I gave the "L.T." to Paige.)

OFFICIAL MEMBER

Jessie   Dilly

Button from striped sweater → DON'T LOSE!

~~Me and~~ Jessie and ~~me~~ I made membership cards for our FROG CLUB in Arts & Crafts. EVERYBODY wants them - even the "Fellowship" girls. I think we're going to need to make MORE.

BUT of course it's not enough to WANT to be in the FROG CLUB you must pass the... I·N·I·T·I·A·T·I·O·N...

USA 32

Daspletosaurus USA 32

32 USA B A L L E T

32 USA Wyoming toad

COOL STAMPS FROM LETTERS I'VE GOTTEN

Julie started a UNICORN CLUB cuz she said my FROG CLUB is dumb cuz frogs are gross (ARE NOT!) But because you can't catch unicorns and play with them, NOBODY wants to join!

★ At dinner (HOT DOGS- YEA!), Sylvia said that at her school some mean kids call her "saliva" (that means "spit"). She acts so cool I didn't think she ever got teased.

TYPICAL FROG DINNER
First, a few EARWIGS and BEETLES, then a couple of FLIES, ANTS and SPIDERS. And for dessert... a SLUG and some WOOD LICE. YUMMY!!

we had a rehearsal for the camp show. Only I did not have to do my act cuz it's a SECRET.

FROG FACT
All toads are
FROGS!!

Everyone wanted me to be on their team for today's Scavenger Hunt cuz #3 on the list was a toad and #11 was a ladybug. They all know I'm GREAT at catching stuff. (I went with Paige and Meredith cuz they REALLY needed me!)

Already did, Dad!

HI SWEETIE!
WE SURE DO MISS YOUR SMILING FACE AROUND HERE! MATT GOT A LETTER FROM YOU TODAY AND HE LET MOM AND ME TAKE A PEEK AT IT. SOUNDS LIKE YOU MIGHT BE A LITTLE HOMESICK. I KNOW THAT A FEW THINGS ARE DIFFERENT FROM WHAT YOU EXPECTED, BUT I'LL BET THAT IF YOU MAKE UP YOUR MIND TO ENJOY CAMP, YOU WILL!

WITH LOVE,
Dad

P.S. HERE IS A LITTLE SPENDING MONEY. I KNOW SHOPPING ALWAYS CHEERS MOM UP! XOXO

My dad always saves frog articles for me!

Today we rode our horses into the woods. Starflight jumps over fallen trees _way_ better than the other horses (who actually just STEP over them). Sylvia fixed the stirrups so my feet don't drag anymore. And Paige helped me braid Starflight's mane! (The other horses' manes are too high to reach.) It looked VERY PRETTY!

Thousands of frogs are killed every year as they try to cross busy roads during their annual migrations to and from breeding areas. It is becoming more common to see signs like the one at left, warning drivers about the migrating amphibians.

★ TOMORROW'S THE BIG SHOW! ★

#9 Use string to tie on slices of cheese for in-line skate pads— GROOVY!

we smell cheese!

#10 If you suspect your friend is wanted by the F.B.I, get her fingerprints on a slice of cheese!

Ah ha!

CLAP CLAP

HA HA HA

CLAP CLAP CLAP

So PLEASE, fellow campers, the next time you are tempted to take a bite of cheese, REMEMBER....

IF PEOPLE WERE MEANT TO EAT CHEESE, WE WOULD BE MICE!

Thank you very much!

I could tell everyone liked _mine_ best, but all the acts were pretty good. Meredith's skit was cute except that Julie got nervous and messed up her lines. (I actually felt SORRY for her.) The "Fellowship" girls do the same thing every year— a dance to ♫♪ Yellow Polka Dot Bikini ♫♪ Robin's act was ALMOST as good as mine! The other "Trail's End" girls threw stuff to her and she juggled it!

(I can't believe the day after tomorrow is PARENTS' DAY! Why, those 3 weeks just FLEW by!)

Next year, I'll do my sword swallowing act and REALLY impress 'em!

Only 1 more day ☹ Parents' Day

"Dee Dee!"

"Matty!"

I bought this bear for Matt at the camp store. → DAKOTA

Mom and Dad don't look one bit older!

Mine were the very first parents to arrive! ☺

"DILLY!"

Mom and Dad met all my friends (and Julie, too). Everyone thought Matt was a cutie! We had FUNNER THAN FUN games and contests all afternoon and an Awards Ceremony at night. I won First Place for horse jumping and for best groomed horse and Second in Nature Study!

Mom and Dad (and Matt) are staying in a hotel tonight and they said I could stay with them, but I wanted to spend the LAST NIGHT with my friends! (M.B. and I switched so I get the TOP bunk tonight!)

1st PLACE

FIRST PLACE

SECOND PLACE

LAST DAY OF CAMP

Hannah gave me this frog charm from her bracelet as a good-bye present!
←

This morning we packed up our trunks and said good-bye. (Jessie and I switched some of our stuff so our parents will <u>HAVE</u> to get us together!) Thank goodness I don't have to say good-bye to Meredith - we get to be together all the way home!

Meredith took this for me. (Mary Beth isn't in the picture cuz she left early this morning - IN A <u>LIMO</u>!)

↑
Hannah's sister <u>DOES</u> look just like her!

FINAL FROG FACT
Most frogs have a small "home range". My camp frogs will spend the winter in the pond's mud and then we'll be able to find them again next year!

Bye Frogs!
(It was kind of sad letting them go.)

Bye Camp Dakota!

Only 344 days until the first day of camp <u>NEXT</u> summer!

Jessie's salamander
↓

HI DILLY

your mom g...
your addres...
write to li...
like li...

Hi Dilly! Do you miss...

Boo
whe...

miss you
without
my dog.

SEE YOU AT HOME! LOVE, MER

Bye, Julie Ann Baldwin   I'll miss you! Bye! Liddy

★letter holder

Don't forget to write to me! Remember: we're sharing a bunk next year, too!
Mary Beth White
32 Centre St.
Newport, R.I.

~Farewell, dear friend... Perhaps next summer we shall be together within the buoys... Best wishes, Robin~

Bye #1 froggirl!

Love, Hannah

Dilly- You are the one who made camp fun for me. Thanks! Love, Jessie
P.S. I only live 2 hours away from you! Hope to see you real soon...

Have a great year!
FROGS RULE! ♥ Paige
U.R. COOL!! Naomi

Liza

Love ya Dilly! Write me! (sbragg@mon.net) Sylvia